Melody's Kooky Cover-Up

A Story About Building Self-Worth

Featuring the Psalty family of characters
created by Ernie and Debby Rettino

Written by Ken Gire
Illustrated by John Dickenson
and Bob Payne

Published by Focus on the Family Publishing/Maranatha! for Kids

P. O. Box 500, Arcadia, CA 91006. Distributed by Word Books, Waco, Texas.

Library of Congress Catalog Card Number 87-80939
ISBN 084-9999-944

It was a bright, sunny day as Melody skipped down the sidewalk. She felt so good inside that she could hardly keep all of her warm feelings in. So they bubbled out as a happy, light-hearted song.

"Good morning, birdies!" she sang as she passed under the trees.

And all her gaily-feathered friends sang their good mornings back to her: "Tweet tweet. . .tweet tweet!"

Moving down the sidewalk, she passed a bookstore window that was filled with all sorts of new children's books.

"Oh my!" she exclaimed as she stopped and gazed in the window. All the books had pretty covers, decorated with drawings in a rainbow of bright colors. She thought to herself as she stared: "They're so shiny, so...so...so beeeyuuutiful."

Then she caught a glimpse of her reflection in the glass.
"Oh," she gasped. She wanted to run and hide, because
she saw how simple and plain she was compared to the
books inside the store. She stepped closer to the window and
took a long hard look at herself. It was enough to make her
cry. She had no bright colors. She had no cute drawings.
And she had no shine. All she had was a very common, very
dull, very ordinary pink cover.

Suddenly her face grew hot. She felt so ugly . . . so unimportant. Her eyes began to fill with tears. And then she dashed off down the sidewalk, crying as she ran.

She stumbled on for blocks and blocks until she was all run out. As she trudged along, her feet felt so heavy. With her head bent down, she passed under some trees with big, leafy branches.

As she did, the birds sang out to greet her: "Tweet tweet. . .tweet tweet!"

But she couldn't sing back. Melody had lost her song.

As she walked, she passed another storefront window. It was a gift shop filled with all kinds of wrapping paper. Some of the paper was covered with purple and orange polka dots, some with blue and yellow stripes. Other paper had pictures of beautiful flowers, colorful balloons or, little furry animals. All of the paper was very, very pretty.

"That's it!" Melody said, snapping her fingers in delight. "I'll get some bright new wrapping paper and make my own book cover!"

So in she went. When she came out of the store, her arms
were filled with all sorts of brightly-colored wrapping
paper, scissors, and plenty of tape.

"Now I can be just like the books in the window!" she
exclaimed.

So she trimmed and cut, folded and taped. It was very hard work, but before long, she had made herself a fancy new book cover. Melody was so excited! She even felt her song starting to return.

Melody walked tall and proud back to the bookstore
window. She couldn't wait till the other books saw her.
However, when she came to the window; all the display
books glared at her with big, long, mean-looking frowns.

"Take a look at that," she overheard one say as he nudged the book next to him.

"Who does she think she is?" uttered another under her breath.

"Look at that kooky-looking book cover," snickered another.

Then they all started to giggle.

Melody couldn't help herself. Starting to cry, she ran away as fast as she could. And as she ran, she tore off her wrapping-paper book cover.

When she reached home, she dashed to her bedroom and threw herself on her bed. She buried her head in the pillow and began to sob.

"I'm so ugly," she said, "and so worthless. Nobody likes me . . . nobody likes me." She cried and cried until she ran out of tears.

Her father Psalty, the singing songbook, heard Melody's sobs and came in to see if she was all right.

"Melody, Melody," he said softly as he bent down to give her a hug. "What's the matter?"

But Melody just sniffled in response.

"Come now, my little booklet, it can't be as bad as all that, can it?"

"Nobody likes me."

"Don't say that, Melody," he said. "We all love you. Rhythm, Harmony, Mom, and I—we all love you very, very much."

"But nobody else does."

"Why do you think that, sweetheart?"

"Because I don't have a new, shiny cover like the books at the store. I'm just plain, old, good-for-nothing me."

He tenderly stroked her hair. "So that's what's bothering you."

Melody nodded without saying anything.

"Sometimes we think our looks are all that matters," Psalty said. "And we sometimes worry too much about what we wear or how we style our hair. But to God, it's what's on the inside that's most important.

"You see, Melody," continued Psalty, "God looks at our hearts. To Him, it's not what's on the book cover that's important; it's what's on the inside that counts."

Melody sat up and began to dry her tears. "You mean He doesn't care whether I have a fancy book cover or not? It doesn't bother Him that I look so . . . so ordinary?"

"Listen to what God says in the Bible and see for yourself," Psalty answered. " 'Don't be concerned about the outward beauty that depends on jewelry, or beautiful clothes, or hair arrangement. Be beautiful inside, in your hearts . . . this is precious to God.' "

Psalty reached over to the bookshelf beside Melody's bed and pulled out a tattered and play-worn little storybook.

"Remember this book?"

Melody nodded with a smile. It was her favorite storybook.

"I remember how much you loved this book from the day your Mom and I gave it to you...how it made you laugh...how it cheered you up no matter how bad you felt. Look how frayed it is around the edges."

He handed the book to her. "Was it the cover that gave you so much joy or the story inside?"

"The story," answered Melody.

Psalty pulled another book from the shelf so Melody could see it. It was a cookbook that her mother Psaltina had given Melody.

"There...look at the mess on the cover of this one!" He pointed to the spots the butter had made and where the cake batter had soaked in and dried. "But you know, honey, it's the recipes inside that gave us the delicious cakes and pies—not the pictures on the outside."

Finally, Psalty took another book from the shelf. "Look at this, Melody," he said. "Here's your first Bible. It just has a plain white cover—nothing fancy. And look at all the finger marks from your eager hands."

He handed the Bible to Melody. "What is it that you love about this book?" he asked.

Melody looked at the Bible and thought. "I love it because it tells about the beautiful story of God's love for the world," she answered.

"God is like a Master Bookmaker, Melody, and you were made to be a special limited edition of one . . . with a special story only you can tell."

Melody's eyes grew big and bright. "And God loves me no matter what I look like on the outside," she said, "because He looks at the inside—at my heart—doesn't He, Dad?"

"That's right, and you have a beautiful heart, my sweet little booklet!"

Then they gave each other a big, warm hug . . . and Melody felt a sudden urge to sing. As the music bubbled up from her toes, she smiled up at her father and began to hum.

"I think . . . yes, my song has returned!" she exclaimed, as she started to sing.

Psalty joined in, and together they marched out of the room singing their favorite sing-along song.